NO AR

S0-AYT-344

Everything You Need To Know About

TEEN FATHERHOOD

Fatherhood brings both extra responsibilities and new joys.

• THE NEED TO KNOW LIBRARY •

Everything You Need To Know About

TEEN FATHERHOOD

Eleanor H. Ayer

THE ROSEN PUBLISHING GROUP, INC.
NEW YORK

Published in 1993, 1995, 1998 by The Rosen Publishing Group, Inc.
29 East 21st Street, New York, NY 10010

Copyright © 1993, 1995, 1998 by The Rosen Publishing Group, Inc.

Revised Edition 1998

Library of Congress Cataloging-in-Publication Data

Ayer, Eleanor H.
    Everything you need to know about teen fatherhood / Eleanor H. Ayer. — rev.
ed.
    (The need to know library)
    Includes bibliographical references and index.
    Summary: Discusses the emotional, physical, and financial concerns involved
with becoming a teenage father and examines the responsibilities and choices
offered by the situation.
        ISBN 0-8239-2842-X
    1. Teenage fathers—United States—Juvenile Literature. 2. Teenage fathers—
United States—Life skills guide—Juvenile literature. 3. Unmarried fathers—United
States—Juvenile literature. [1. Teenage fathers.] I. Title.
HQ756.7.A94   1993
306.874'2'0835—dc20   92-39945
                                                                       CIP
                                                                        AC

Manufactured in the United States of America
                                                                       92-39945
                                                                        CIP
                                                                         AC

Contents

Introduction: Thinking About Teen Fatherhood

Teen fatherhood is an important issue in our nation. Approximately 7 percent of teen males have fathered children. These fathers face many serious challenges. They must make decisions that greatly affect their lives and those of their families and children. The purpose of this book is to help young fathers understand the economic and emotional questions that face them now and that will continue to face them in the future. If you are reading this book you may already be a teen father or may soon become one. Or you may not yet be a father but want to know more about the issues.

Choosing Together

If you are old enough to have sex, you are old enough to act with responsibility. If you are in a relationship, you and your girlfriend need to make some choices together. Although it sounds unromantic and maybe even embarrassing, it is imortant to discuss your physical relationship and agree in advance how far it will go. If you both choose to have sex, take the time to make good choices to protect yourselves and your future. Respect your body and that of your girl-friend. A girl can become pregnant the first time she has sex and any time after that, even if she is having her period. If you are not prepared to have a child, then you both need to prevent it. *Contraception* is not just "her problem."

Unprotected sex can also expose you to sexually transmitted diseases (STD). *AIDS* is the most serious. There is currently no cure for AIDS. You can also get syphilis, gonorrhea, herpes, chlamydia, or other dis-eases from having sex with someone who is infected. You cannot tell from looking at a person if he or she has an STD. Some people may not know they have one or may not be truthful about it.

You and your girlfriend can protect yourselves from STDs and pregnancy. The safest and surest way is absti-nence, which means not having sex. If you choose abstinence, make it easier for yourself by avoiding situ-ations that can lead to sex. Date in groups, instead of alone. Avoid staying in a car or house alone with your girlfriend. Avoid long sessions of kissing or touching each other. Decide together beforehand that sex will not be part of your relationship. This will make it easier to abstain.

If you do choose to have sex, take care of yourself and your girlfriend by practicing safer sex. Safer sex is low risk but not risk-free. This means you will have to use at least a *condom*, a rubber casing that is rolled over an erect penis (preferably, one coated with nonoxynol-9, which helps protect against AIDS). This method is used to protect you from unwanted pregnancy and from infection by an STD. However, a condom alone is not 100 percent effective.

The Choice of Fatherhood

For boys, being sexually active carries with it the possibility of fatherhood. Fatherhood is a major life change. If you are or soon will be a father, you may be confused or have doubts about what fatherhood means. Ask men who were teen fathers about their experiences and if they have any regrets. Discuss your feelings and beliefs with your parents, a counselor, or a religious leader. If you are uncomfortable discussing these issues with someone you know, contact an organization such as Planned Parenthood. Several such organizations are listed at the end of this book. In addition, a number of communities have support groups for teen fathers and programs to encourage them to be responsible fathers while they continue to go to school or work.

Today, the role of teen fathers is seen much differently than it was in the past. Society once discouraged the father from becoming part of his baby's life unless the parents married. Today the teen father is often encouraged, even expected to participate in the care and development of his child. Many social programs and organizations have begun to reevaluate the role of the teen father, recognizing the important bond between father and child. Statistics show that in general, children

Couples need to act responsibly about decisions that involve sex.

raised without fathers encounter more emotional, social, educational, and health problems than those from two-parent families and are more likely to live in poverty.

With the freedom to make your own choices comes the responsibility to accept the consequences of those choices. You will sometimes make poor choices; everybody does. But you can learn from your mistakes.

The choices you make will affect you, your partner, and your child. Be prepared to stand behind your choices. One of the goals of this book is to help you make the decisions that are right for all of you.

Talking to parents may be helpful in reaching a decision about an unexpected pregnancy.

Chapter 1

Coping with the News

It was Saturday morning, and Mark's head was full of thoughts about the coming school year. He would be a junior this September, and he had some exciting decisions to make about his future. Would he apply to junior college? Would he look for a job? He had always liked the idea of going into business, and his uncle said he seemed to have the knack for it. His thoughts were interrupted by the ringing telephone. It was Celia, his girlfriend. "We need to talk," she said. "Can we meet this afternoon?" Mark knew something must be wrong. Could she be upset that he had cancelled on her for going to the movies on Monday?

Mark and Celia had been together for a year and a half. They had even talked about getting married, but both of them had known that the possibility of that was many years ahead. Now, sitting in the park on a *sunny bench, she told him she was pregnant.*

"Pregnant?!" Mark whispered in shock. He sat stunned at first. Then he became angry, angry at Celia and at himself. Why had this happened to them? Hadn't they always been careful? What had they done wrong? He saw that his response upset her. He tried to talk with Celia, but she could only cry. He felt afraid, confused, and very much alone. He thought she must too. What were they going to do?

When you first found out that you were going to be a father, you probably felt a lot of different emotions. You may have been angry at the mother for getting pregnant even though it is unlikely that she intended to. You may have been angry at yourself for allowing the pregnancy to happen. Maybe you didn't take the proper precautions, or maybe you were careless. You may have been angry at the world, or at fate.

You may also have felt shock. Maybe, like Mark, you took precautions but were unlucky. Probably you didn't expect to become a father when you became intimate with the soon-to-be mother of your child.

Often shock leads to another response: denial. Someone can't handle the news and so refuses to accept it. Denial is the "ignore it and it will go away" school of thought. But in the case of a pregnancy denial only wastes time you could be using to make good decisions.

Recently, an unmarried teenage couple from Delaware killed their newborn child because they were afraid. Both were arrested and charged with murder. Had they faced the difficult question of what to do about their unexpected pregnancy earlier, rather than denying it, they could have made a better decision.

Most boys are afraid when they discover their girl-friend is pregnant. You may feel that your life is out of control. You may worry about how your parents will take the news, how you are going to deal with the preg-nancy, and what your friends will say. You may feel overwhelmed, afraid that nothing will work out. All of these emotions working together can create a feeling of confusion. You may feel lost.

Sometimes these feelings are followed by another, acceptance of what has taken place. Maybe you and your girlfriend weren't ready for the pregnancy, and maybe you aren't ready for what's going to happen to your life because of it. But your girlfriend did get preg-nant, and now you have to deal with it. You accept what has happened and know that you will have to tackle difficult questions.

If you're lucky, you might begin to feel another emo-tion: joy. Perhaps you are or may soon be ecstatic about the idea of becoming a father.

You may be experiencing all or none of these feel-ings, or some combination. But whatever you're feel-ing, it's time for you to sit down with your girlfriend. It's important to ask her how she feels and to listen carefully as she tells you. It's also important to let her know how you feel. Be honest. The more open you can both be about your feelings, the better you will be prepared to decide together what to do now.

Family

It's a hard truth, but usually the best decision you can make is to tell your parents about the pregnancy. They probably won't be overjoyed at first, but they can help you make your decision. They can also offer you advice.

There is no easy way to tell your parents about a pregnancy. Even if you and your girlfriend are over-flowing with happiness about it, you may be afraid that your parents will be upset. But it is important to tell them, and the sooner you do, the better.

The best way to tell your parents is to be honest. Tell them how you feel about the pregnancy. If you have made any decisions, tell them what they are.

Your parents may not take the news well. Or maybe your parents are calm when they learn of the pregnancy, but your girlfriend's parents are not. Some parents try to take control of the situation and pay no attention to what you have to say.

It may help to talk to another adult before talking with your parents, because that person can help you know what questions, concerns, and feelings your parents might have. He or she can also help you sort through your alternatives. That way, when you do talk to your parents you will have a better sense of your options and your feelings. A trusted teacher, school counselor, or religious leader may be a great help to you. Don't be ashamed to ask for help.

Be honest with yourself about whether you are ready to raise your child. If your parents want you to keep the child and you don't think you are ready for such a heavy responsibility, tell them so. Work with your girlfriend, your family, and perhaps a social worker to find alternatives. Or if your parents want you to give up the baby and you want to keep it, don't just give in to your parents' wishes; think seriously about the arguments for and against what you want to do. If you still feel strongly that you are ready to be a good parent, stand firm and demonstrate that you are serious. Take the time to figure out how you will be able to manage raising a child.

You are responsible for your decisions. Although you are still young, you do have a say in what happens to you and your child.

Chapter 2

Deciding What's Right for You

Years ago, when an unmarried girl got pregnant, there was only one choice: marriage. People thought marriage was "the only honorable thing to do." Today marriage is one of several options. Whatever you decide, it is important to remember that your girlfriend may or may not agree. It is an issue you need to try to work out together.

Considering Abortion

If the pregnancy was unplanned and you have no desire or ability to raise a child, *abortion* may be a choice. It is a quick way to end a pregnancy. It is the choice of many teens who feel they are not ready to be parents. But abortion is a serious and difficult decision. It is not a form of birth control. Abortion means actively choosing not to bring a child into the world.

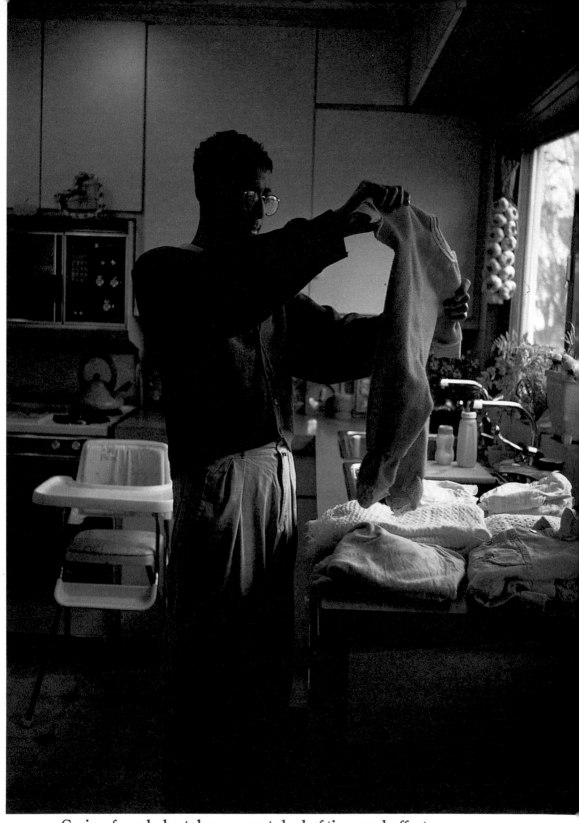

Caring for a baby takes a great deal of time and effort.

This is a choice that will have lasting consequences.

During the first three months of pregnancy, the girl and her family may choose abortion even if the father does not agree. Later in the pregnancy, the doctor or even the state may become involved in the decision. Abortion restrictions differ from state to state.

Adoption

Many teens who are against abortion but are not ready or able to raise a child choose *adoption*. "We wanted him to have a chance to grow up, but we knew we couldn't give him a good home. There are lots of couples waiting to adopt, so we figured he'd have a good chance," said one teen father.

Adoption, too, can be painful. "I was glad to have it all behind me," recalls Dan, who was seventeen when he became a father. That was twenty years ago. "I'm glad I did what I did at the time, but it haunts me to think that I have a twenty-year-old daughter out there somewhere."

In some states, a father has equal rights with a mother in deciding on adoption. In other states, the father has no say. Check with your local social services office to find out about your rights.

There are many things to consider if you are helping to make the adoption decision :

Adoption agencies If adoption is your choice but you don't know where to begin, look in the yellow pages under "Adoption Agencies." People at the agencies know the laws about adoption for your state.

They know families who want to adopt a baby. They can help you through the difficult legal and personal steps involved in adoption.

To be sure that you're working with a good agency, check with a social worker. Call more than one agency. Find out how long each has been in business. Ask to see proof that they are licensed by the state. You do not want to give your child to an organization that may not care about the child's welfare.

Private adoption You or a trusted adult may know of a couple who would like to adopt your baby. In this case, you do not have to go through an agency. If a private adoption is your choice, be sure you work with a reputable lawyer to draw up the proper legal papers.

Signing the papers During pregnancy, you or your girlfriend may change your mind about adoption. This is not uncommon. You can wait until the baby is born to sign the adoption papers. Adoption is not final until the papers are signed.

Knowing what you want You may be under pressure from parents, counselors, or even the adoption agency to give up your baby. But you and your girlfriend are the ones who must make the decision. No one else should decide for you.

Adoption is a tough decision. If you use an agency, you will probably never see your baby after it is born. You will not know who the adopting parents are. This is done to protect their privacy as well as the child's. After the adoption is final, there is no going

It is important to discuss adoption with trustworthy people who are well informed about it.

back. All your life you may wonder if you did the right thing. That is why it is so important to take your time and make your decision carefully. Find out all the facts. Talk with as many people as you can. Then trust in yourself that you will make the right decision.

Marriage

When Rick and Jennifer learned they were going to have a baby, they made the decision to get married. "We were happy, but very scared. We were against abortion. Both of us wanted to be with the child. At the time," recalls Rick, "I thought that was the right decision. Still, I was worried. I didn't know how we were going to make it."

Teen marriage is usually tense and stressful. Lack of money, job skills, and education can bring problems to a marriage. So can the pressure to be a good parent and father. Many teen marriages are not able to survive this stress. The rate of divorce for teens is very high. A girl married at seventeen is twice as likely to divorce as a girl married at eighteen or nineteen. If she waits until she is twenty-five, the chances that her marriage will last are four times better.

Living Together/Living Apart

You and your girlfriend may choose to have the baby but not to marry. You may decide to live together without being married, or to live apart and share the responsibility of raising your child.

On the plus side, you can become a father without the pressure of becoming a husband at the same time. You can help raise your child and watch it grow and develop.

On the minus side, you have made no commitment to the child's mother. She has made none to you.

Either of you could walk away at any time.

If you are not married, you need to be sure that your rights as a father are protected. In many states, your name will not appear on the child's birth certificate unless the mother requests it. If you want to be named legally as the father, you must have a paternity test. If the test is positive, you are the father and your name may be added to the birth certificate. This gives you legal rights to your child.

The legal father must pay child support even if he has never been married to the mother. Child support begins when the baby is born and usually continues until he or she is eighteen. Even if the father is still in school, he must make child-support payments. The court may require him to make only part of each payment. But he has to pay the rest as soon as he is able.

Father as a Single Parent

Choosing to raise a baby alone is a choice few teen fathers make. But it may be the right choice for you. Being "Mr. Mom" will not be easy, but it can be rewarding. Before you make your decision, ask yourself these questions:

- Do you *want* to learn how to care for a baby?
- Can you handle the double load of working and being a full-time single parent?
- What friends or family members can support you emotionally?
- Who can care for the child while you are away from home?

- What kind of support can you expect from the mother?
- Are you ready to make this important lifetime commitment?
- What if your girlfriend comes back in a year and wants to take the child? How can you be sure you and the child are protected?

A Difficult Decision

Whatever your choice, it must be the one that you think is right. Talk with many people. Try to find an older man who became a father as a teenager.

Counselors at schools, churches, hospitals, and social services agencies are trained to help people solve difficult problems.

Try to listen to your parents or older family members, too. Even if the pregnancy has made them angry, they can be helpful. Age and experience help people to make better decisions. Your parents know you well. They may surprise you by offering some very good advice.

It may be necessary to get a full-time or part-time job in order to fulfill the responsibilities of fatherhood.

Chapter 3

Growing Up on Fast Forward

Becoming a teenage dad means growing up in a big hurry. Suddenly, you face a huge responsibility. Not long ago, you were a child yourself. You needed a safe home where people loved you, clean clothes and nourishing food, and guidance to grow up to be a good person. Now you must provide those things for your own child.

A Question of Paternity

Sometimes there is a reason to question who is the baby's father. It was that way with Jose and Angela. "That's one reason I ran," Jose admits. "Sure, Angela and I had been having sex. But I knew she had been with other guys, too. One of them could have been the father."

Jose got scared when Angela started pressing him

to marry her. "She told me that even if I didn't, I still had to pay child support for the next eighteen years. I didn't even have a job. I panicked."

A paternity test could have helped Jose answer the question of fatherhood. This is a medical test in which DNA from the mother, father, and baby are compared. If the test is negative, it shows that this man could not have been the baby's father. If the test is positive, it indicates that there is a 99.9 percent probability that he is the father. It is possible to have a paternity test before the baby is born, but this is much more expensive. If there is any question in your mind that you might not be the father, you will want to have a paternity test. A doctor or clinic can tell you how to arrange for it.

Accepting Your Responsibility

When you choose to raise your baby, you make a commitment. You promise to give the child love, guidance, money, and a good home for nearly eighteen years. You promise to raise your child in the very best way you can. There's no backing out of fatherhood.

Accepting such a big responsibility can make you scared and uncertain. This is natural. But you are not alone. Your girlfriend is probably just as scared and uncertain as you are. She needs your *moral support* right now, and you need hers. If raising your child together is your choice, you must both make the commitment to do a good job. Being a good dad is just as big a responsibility as being a good mom.

Many Teen Fathers

If you are a teen father, you are not alone. There are many teen fathers. Every year in the United States, 1 million teenage girls become pregnant, and 550,000 babies are born to teen mothers. Each of these babies has a father, and many (although not all) are teens. About one of out of every seven babies has a teen for a mother.

The statistics concerning teen fatherhood are not encouraging. Only one in five fathers associated with those 550,000 births continues to support his child financially or emotionally. Only one couple out of twenty marries, and those couples that do marry have a divorce rate that is higher than average. The couples who stick together often have more problems than couples who are in their twenties or older. Babies born to teenage mothers have a higher chance of dying before their first birthday than those born to adult mothers, and teenage married couples make up a higher percentage of poor people than adult married couples.

However, those are just the statistics. There are also the exceptions. If you decide to become a teenage father, you may have to work harder to beat the odds against you. But if you are determined, you can have a happy, loving, and healthy family.

Regular visits to the doctor are important during pregnancy.

Chapter 4

Preparing for Childbirth

Anormal pregnancy usually lasts nine months. Most people need that long to adjust to the idea of parenthood. As a future father, you may need to think about practical things like getting a job, making a *budget*, fixing up baby's room, and just finding the time to be a dad.

Mom, meanwhile, is learning to adjust to her changing body. Every pregnancy is different. Some women feel very few side effects, others may feel sick or uncomfortable. There is no way to know in advance how a pregnancy will progress.

Prenatal Care

Every pregnant woman needs *prenatal* (before birth) care. Without the proper care, the baby may be born with serious health problems. It may die during the first year.

Most doctors advise one checkup a month during the first seven months of pregnancy. The mother should go every two weeks in the eighth month, and once a week during the last month. The father is welcome at all prenatal visits. You or the mother's parents may have insurance to cover the cost of a private doctor. If not, check with your social services office to see about Medicaid or a low-cost clinic.

Good prenatal care means that the mother needs to eat a well-balanced diet and not harm her body in any way. As the father, you can help Mom follow some smart rules for pregnancy.

- Exercise regularly.
- Avoid alcohol and drugs. Even aspirin can cause harm to the unborn baby.
- Avoid drinks with caffeine, such as coffee, tea, and soda, whenever possible.
- Avoid smoking and smoky environments.

The Three Stages of Pregnancy

If you divide the nine months of pregnancy by three, you have three *trimesters*, each three months long. During the first trimester, a woman may feel nauseated much of the time. The changes going on in her body can cause heartburn, constipation, dizziness, or other symptoms. Since her body is literally creating another person day by day, she may be hungry often and feel fatigued. Rest is important.

Along with the changes in her body, you may notice changes in her moods. She may be happy one minute and upset the next. This is normal. She may be irritable much of the time. For many women, it is not easy to be pregnant. Try to be understanding.

During the second trimester, many women do not feel as sick or tired as they did earlier. The legs, breasts, and abdomen (belly) swell as the pregnancy begins to show. During this period, the *fetus*—the unborn baby—starts to move. You may occasionally feel this movement when you put your hand on the mother's abdomen. A doctor can let you hear the fetal heartbeat. By now the pregnancy is probably very real to both of you.

In the third trimester, the fetus may become quite active. All the extra weight may make the mother tire more easily. Routine jobs may be more difficult for her. It is important for the mother's health and the baby's that she get a lot of rest.

As *delivery* day draws nearer, the mother may become worried. How painful is this going to be? Will the baby be OK? Am I ready to take my child home and care for it? As father, your job is to provide moral support. Try to understand how she feels. Let her know that she's not alone.

Although your body has not changed during pregnancy, you may find that your moods are up and down, too. Try to relax. You can make it.

Getting Ready for the Big Day

Childbirth classes can help you prepare for delivery. Most hospitals or clinics offer classes to help both

The Three Stages of Pregnancy

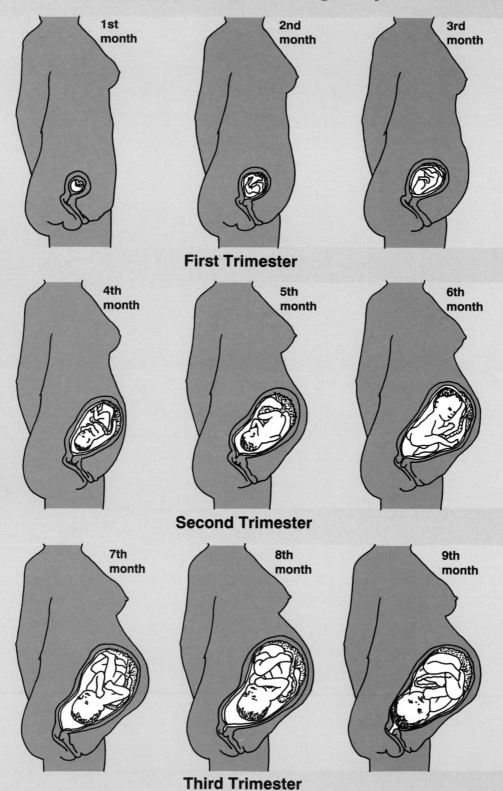

1st month   2nd month   3rd month

First Trimester

4th month   5th month   6th month

Second Trimester

7th month   8th month   9th month

Third Trimester

mother and father understand the process of pregnancy and childbirth.

You will learn about the different ways of having a baby. Perhaps you will decide to have your child at home, with the help of a *midwife*. This person is usually a woman. Although she is not a doctor, she is very experienced in delivering babies.

You may choose the *Lamaze* method of childbirth. This is one way of having a baby without *anesthetics* or drugs. Both of you get involved in learning how the mother should breathe and push during delivery. Dad is the coach, helping Mom to relax and giving her encouragement. If Mom forgets how to breathe properly or when it's time to push, it's up to Dad to remind her. With the Lamaze method, you can have your baby in a hospital or at home.

Sometimes—depending on the health of the mother or the fetus—*cesarean birth* may be necessary. This means the baby is delivered by surgery. A doctor performs an operation to remove the baby through an opening in the mother's abdomen. Some hospitals allow fathers to be in the room during this kind of birth.

If you have any questions, write them down. Your childbirth class instructors are prepared to discuss all of your concerns.

Keeping in touch with friends may help with the pressures of new responsibilities.

Chapter 5

Dealing with the Outside World

For Rick, the hardest part of becoming a father at eighteen was "not being able to do things with my friends. I didn't have any time. I lost contact with them." Some expectant fathers work, some go to school, some do both. What little free time you have is usually spent with your girlfriend. There are many things you must do to prepare for the new baby.

You may also find that you have less in common with friends now. They probably have no idea what it's like to be an expectant father. They may not understand why you don't party as you used to. Even your best friend may suddenly seem *immature* to you. You're headed in different directions. You are facing adult responsibility.

Juggling a Job

Whether or not you've ever had a job, it may be time to get one now. Most teenagers can't count on their parents to support them and their new family. Your job may pay only *minimum wage* to start. That's okay. Most employers don't pay higher wages unless you have experience or an education. Chances are you have neither.

But you do have two things in your favor: a lot of energy, and a good reason to work. These are your strong points. Take advantage of them. Show your employer that you are willing to do more than is asked of you. Show him or her that you are eager to learn and improve in your job. Let your boss know that you have a family on the way and that you're trying your best to support it. If you show the boss that you're different, you will be treated differently. Soon you could be moving up the employment ladder-and up the pay scale.

If you're having trouble finding a job, don't get discouraged. Keep reading the classified ads and talking to people. Ask your school counselor for advice. Talk with a social worker. Go to the state unemployment office in you area. Sign up at a temporary agency. Most local phone books list these agencies under "Employment" in the Yellow Pages. Unemployment is at a low level these days, and there are usually jobs for people who are willing to start at the bottom, work hard, and improve.

Staying in School

Just because you have found a job doesn't mean you should quit school. It won't be easy, but try to find a way to finish your education. A high school education is extremely important. Without one, it's much harder to find a good job and keep it.

It's easier to finish school before the baby is born. After that it's much harder to find the time (or a quiet place) to study. Perhaps you can work nights and go to school during the day. If not, look into *GED* (General Equivalency Diploma) classes at night. Your high school will have information.

Getting your high school diploma will make you feel good about yourself. You'll be proud of having reached your goal. Your girlfriend will be proud of you, too. But most important, you'll be setting a good example for your child. By finishing school, you're showing your child that you think education is important. Your child will be much more likely to follow your example.

Handling All the Pressure

Pressure, commitments, responsibilities—how do you handle them all? Talking things over with a social worker or counselor may help. If you are more comfortable talking with a family member or religious leader, that's good, too. Most adults you trust will be glad to offer helpful ideas. And the more ideas you have, the better decisions you can make.

A monthly budget gives you a sense of control over your finances.

Chapter 6

Balancing the Budget

As a responsible father, you should put your family's needs first. Money that is supposed to buy baby food cannot be spent on a new cassette tape. You must be sure that baby and mother have a secure place to live. This means paying the rent, heat, electric, and other important bills on time.

Even if you are not living together, you need to help support your child. The law says you must pay a certain portion of your child's bills. And as a good father, you should *want* to do this.

It's hard enough to support yourself. It's even harder when you're trying to support a child. How can you make ends meet? How do you know what to pay for first? By being very careful in the way you spend your money. You must make a plan—*a budget*—and follow that plan very closely.

Making a Budget

There are two sides to every budget: money that comes in and money that goes out. What comes in is your income. Income is any money you receive from wages, interest on an account, gifts, or other sources. What goes out are your expenses. This is the money you spend to pay the bills, start your savings, or buy the things you want.

How do you set up a budget? For many teens, a paycheck is the only income. But some have other sources. Your parents may help by lending you money. Perhaps you qualify for food stamps or other government programs; talk to a school counselor or other adult about this. Make a list of all your income sources. Add up your monthly income from each source and write down the total.

Now list all your monthly expenses. You may want to use the sample budget on page 41 as a guide. *Be honest with yourself.* Don't leave off "Entertainment" if you *know* you're planning to go to the movies. If you're going to stick to your budget, it has to be truthful. Later you may decide to cut some expenses. But for now, list all of them.

When you have listed all your expenses, add up the total. How does it compare to your total income? If you have more expenses than income, it's time to make some choices. Decide which expenses are not really necessary. Instead of cutting out one whole section, try cutting down a little in several sections. The idea is to *balance* the budget, to have expenses match income.

Setting a Little Aside

One of the most important parts of your budget is "Savings." Each month, set aside a regular amount of money for savings. It may be as little as $25. But try to save a regular amount *each month*. Increase that amount as often as you can. Never let savings be the item you cut out of your budget.

If you put your savings into a bank account, you won't be as tempted to spend it. When extra money is needed, work some overtime if you can. Do odd jobs for people. Draw money from savings only for emergencies.

Sample Monthly Budget

Income		Expenses	
Regular paychecks:	$____	Rent:	$____
Welfare or Social Services:	$____	Heat:	$____
Family contribution:	$____	Electricity:	$____
Other income:	$____	Water:	$____
		Phone:	$____
TOTAL INCOME:	$____	Food:	$____
		Clothing:	$____
		Health care:	$____
		Transportation:	$____
		Child care:	$____
		Entertainment:	$____
		Savings:	$____
		Other expenses:	$____
		TOTAL EXPENSES:	$____

What If You Still Can't Make It?

Rick and Jennifer tried their best. But there were times when they just couldn't make it. "Money was very tight," Rick remembers. What do you do when your income doesn't cover your expenses? How do you manage when you've cut everything out of the budget that you can?

"We had to borrow from Jennifer's mother once in a while," Rick recalls. "For a time, we had to live with her parents. Our apartment was too expensive. Those months were hard, but we were hopeful that better days would come."

While they were living with Jennifer's parents, Rick looked for a smaller apartment. He found one that was not as expensive as the first. Spending less on rent gave them more money to pay their other bills. "It took about six months for us to get back on our feet. But we did get there."

Don't be afraid to ask for help. It doesn't mean you're weak or that you're a failure. If you're working hard and trying your best, that's all you can do. In the meantime, don't be too proud. If there are people who are willing to help you, let them. Someday, you may be the one who can offer help to someone else.

Chapter 7

Bringing the Baby Home

"Proud" and "happy." Those are the words many teenage dads use when they talk about seeing their babies for the first time. If you stay with the mom during delivery, you may be the first to hold your baby after birth. This is a special time you will never forget.

Enjoy those few days in the hospital. It is a good time to become familiar with your new baby. You have lots of help around, too. Once baby comes home, he or she is all yours! There are no nurses to give bottles or change diapers. It's your job then—a job for you and Mom.

Paying for the Birth

The cost of prenatal care and delivery can be very expensive. Find out well in advance of the baby's birth if you or your parents have health insurance. It is important to know what services are covered. In preparing your budget you'll need to know if you are paying all or part of the medical bills or just the cost of the insurance itself.

Most births are normal, without problems for mother or baby. Hospital stays are usually one or two days. But sometimes delivery can become long and difficult. Or the baby may be *premature*—born before the full nine months. In premature babies, the lungs or other parts of the body may not be fully developed. This can cause severe health problems and can require the baby to remain in the hospital much longer.

That is why prenatal doctor visits are especially important. They alert you to potential problems and help you prepare.

Preparing the House for Baby

Before you bring the baby home, you will need to shop for supplies and furniture. Maybe you have relatives or friends who can lend you some of the big items, such as a crib or stroller. If not, garage sales or thrift shops are good places to look. Here is a partial list of what you need:

Furniture A full-size or porta-crib with a properly fitting mattress. *Be sure your crib meets safety requirements.* A waterproof pad helps keep the mattress clean and dry. You'll also need a safe place to lay the baby down while you change its diapers. A small dresser with a wide top can double as a changing table and a place to store baby's clothes.

Bringing baby home is an exciting moment for the family.

Baby Carriers Car seats are required by law in every state. They are the best way to keep baby safe in a moving vehicle. A newborn will need an infant-size car seat. You may also want a pack for carrying baby on your chest or back and a stroller.

Food The mother may decide to nurse the baby—feed it with milk from her breasts. If she chooses not to nurse, you will need to buy formula and nursing bottles from a store. Formula is a liquid like mother's milk. During the first few weeks, the only food most babies need is breast milk or formula. Breast-feeding is less expensive than bottle-feeding. But some mothers, especially those who are working or in school, find it hard to nurse their babies.

Diapers You can choose either cloth diapers or disposable diapers. Disposable diapers are more comfortable for baby. They pollute the environment, but so do the bleach and detergent needed to clean cloth diapers.

Bath Supplies It's very important to keep baby's head and neck supported during baths. A thick piece of sponge in the sink or tub makes a good cushion. Some people like to bathe a newborn baby in a small plastic tub. You will also want to get a mild shampoo and soap.

Clothing Most babies stay in sleepers the first few months of life. You'll also need "onesies" (one-piece bodysuits), socks, undershirts, bibs, and pants. For outdoors, dress the baby as warmly as you would dress. Don't forget a hat to keep sun and cold away from baby's head.

Receiving blankets These are small, soft, light-weight blankets. Infants like to be wrapped snugly in them.

Toys Babies like to look at brightly colored things that move. For an infant, objects that hang above the crib (like a mobile) are good.

Still, attention and affection from loving parents is needed most of all.

A Change in Schedule

Remember, having a baby is hard work. Mom may still be weak and tired for a while. She'll need more help at first. Newborns need care twenty-four hours a day. Every few hours, day or night, it's feeding time. In between, the baby may need to be held, changed, rocked, and entertained.

Having a baby in the house changes everyone's schedule. There don't seem to be enough hours in the day. It's important for you and the mother to share the duties around the house as well as taking care of the baby.

It may help to set up a schedule. Decide who will care for the baby during which times of the day. This will give you a regular time with your child. If Mom is always the one who feeds, changes, or plays with the baby, your son or daughter may form a stronger bond with her than with you. That can make you feel like an outsider. And it may cause problems between you and the baby's mother. You, too, can learn to care for a new baby. It just takes a little practice and a lot of love.

Taking turns with feeding will relieve the mother's schedule
and add to the feeling of closeness for the father.

Making room for a third person in your life is not
easy, especially when that person needs constant
attention. It's important to remember that Mom and
Dad need time together without the baby. And each of
you also needs time alone. Discuss it together, and
arrange times for each of you to be alone. You will
both be better parents if you make the time to rest.

48

What If Baby's Home Is Not Your Home?

Darian wanted to help raise his son. But he and Shawna didn't want to get married. "We both lived with our parents. Since the houses weren't far apart, it was easy to share time with him. We agreed the baby would live with Shawna. During the day, she would go to school and I would keep him. Since I worked nights, that made things easy."

Darian bought the diapers and food he would need while the baby was at his house. Shawna bought supplies for her home. When a big expense like a doctor visit came along, they shared the cost.

Their baby is three months old now. "So far it's worked out great," they both agree. "We don't have to put him in day care, and we each get to watch him grow." But they realize that things could get more complex as he gets older. "When he starts needing *discipline*, for example, it will be hard for him if we each set different rules," Darian says. He's also worried about what would happen if either he or Shawna had to move. "It would be real tough only seeing him once in a while. I think about that a lot. I don't know what I'd do."

Darian and Shawna are able to talk and plan together what they think is best for their son even though they do not live together. They can express their feelings and concerns to each other. In the future this may help them make decisions for them and their child.

A father's guidance and support become more important as the child grows.

Chapter 8

Being a Father

If you don't like your car, you can trade it in. When a husband and wife no longer love each other, they may get divorced. But fatherhood is forever. Unless you choose adoption or abortion, your child is yours for the rest of your life. Even if you do not live together, your child is still your responsibility. If you accept that responsibility and do the best job you can of raising your child, it can be very rewarding.

Help in Becoming a Good Parent

Many parts of parenting may seem natural to you. No one will need to tell you to pick up the baby when it is crying. But there will be times when you don't know what to do.

If your child keeps crying and crying, how do you know when to call the doctor? What do you do when your baby wakes in the middle of the night with a

high fever? Is your child developing normally? These
and hundreds of other questions, have worried new
parents for many generations.

Many fine books are available, including the very
reassuring *Baby and Child Care* by Dr. Benjamin
Spock. Others are listed at the end of this book.

After the Newness Wears Off

During the first few weeks, the responsibility and
challenge of fatherhood are exciting. But after those
first few weeks, the newness begins to wear off. The
routine is the same day after day. Caring for your
baby may not seem like fun any longer. You may feel
trapped. At times like these, it is important to reach
out to others and to make time for yourself.

When fatherhood starts to seem like a burden, try
changing your routine. Even a small change can make
a big difference. When you get tense, put the baby in
the stroller and go for a walk. The fresh air and
change of scenery may be good for both of you. Do
something with your child that's fun for you, too, like
taking a drive or spending an afternoon at the beach.
Baby can fit into your life. You don't have to give up
all your activities. Plan ahead when you want to
include the baby in your fun. If you don't want to
take the baby, leave it with someone responsible.

Expressing Your Anger

Anger is an important emotion, but it needs to be
expressed in a healthy manner. How you handle your

It can be fun to include your child in activities you enjoy with your friends.

anger will greatly affect your child's well-being.

Teenage parents are more likely to abuse their children than older parents. Teens have more trouble dealing with their emotions. Don't be a part of the child-abuse statistics. Learn how to recognize and control your anger.

There are times when every parent loses patience with a child. Babies can cry a lot, especially those who suffer from colic—sharp pains in the stomach and abdomen. Toddlers like to do things over and over—even after they have been told no. You may feel like screaming and striking out. *But never hit your child in anger.* If you begin to feel that you might lose control of your anger, stop and give yourself a chance to cool down. Walk into the next room, or call a friend for help. Give yourself time to think.

Parents who were abused when they were children are more likely to abuse their own kids. This means that if you were abused as a child, you have to try twice as hard to control your anger. You may not have been taught healthy ways to express how you are feeling. You can learn these. In the meantime, if you begin to feel angry, take a deep breath and count to ten. This will help you clear your head. Call a friend or relative. Sometimes just describing what happened and how you feel makes a big difference. Try to remember how scared you felt as a child when your mom or dad was hurting you.

Very young children do not *try* to be bad. They may need something they cannot express. Try holding your child, rocking it, taking it for a ride in the stroller, or talking quietly to it. It may take a few minutes. Be patient. Both you and the child will probably settle down.

If you feel you have a problem controlling your anger when you are around your child, seek help. Contact parenting organizations (see pp. 60–61), or talk to a counselor or social worker There is no need to feel embarrassed. You are not alone, and you can end the cycle of child abuse. You are helping yourself and your child, and that is a positive thing.

Setting a Good Example

In the eyes of a child, Mom and Dad are probably the most important people in the world. As children begin the job of sorting out right from wrong, they look to their parents for answers. "Is it OK to hit someone when I'm mad?" If Dad does it, the child will probably decide it's OK. But if Dad keeps his temper and settles his argument by talking, the child may decide that this is the best way.

Children learn by copying. Look at your own behavior. If you don't want your child to drink alcohol or use drugs, avoid them yourself. If you want your child to do well in school, let him or her know that you think education is important. Turn off the television and pick up a newspaper. Have books around your home and read to your child. What the child sees you doing, he or she may imitate.

As Your Child Grows Older

A father often finds that he becomes more important in his child's life as the child grows older and increasingly independent.

As your child gets older, you may find more ways for the two of you to be together. Time with Dad is special to a young child. Take time to enjoy your child and to have fun. Play ball, wrestle, go on picnics, take a walk, make dinner, watch movies together-whatever the two of you like to do. Even doing chores together can be fun.

Time spent reading to your child is very special for both of you.

Beating the Odds

It's not going to be easy. Statistics say the road is rough for teenage parents and especially hard on their children. Children born to parents under seventeen are three times as likely to die as those born to parents who are older. The divorce rate for parents under seventeen is three times greater than for those who have their first child after age twenty. Fewer than 4 percent of single mothers receive any money from the baby's father, which mean their children are more likely to live in poverty.

Making a Wise Decision

Don't be forced into fatherhood. Before you become sexually active, think about the lifetime commitment you may be making. Be certain that you want to be a father. Be sure you understand what it takes to raise a child. Ask yourself honestly if you are willing to do it. Think about the things you probably will be giving up, like dating, partying, school, and the freedom to be on your own. Are you ready to tie yourself down? Are you ready to put the needs of your girlfriend or wife and your child first? Are you able to provide for your new family?

Even if you answer yes to these questions, there will be tough times. There are no easy routes for teenage dads. You must be willing to make sacrifices. You must be ready to work hard. Above all, you must commit yourself to raising your child, being there for him or her day after day, year after year.

Until recently, there has been very little help for teen fathers who want to share in raising their children. Most programs have been geared to teen mothers. But things are changing. New programs are available for fathers (see pp. 60–61).

You are not alone. There is help. It will not be easy, but with courage, love for your child, and the support of others, you can be a good father.

Glossary

abortion A natural or medical way of ending a pregnancy.

adoption Process of taking the child of other parents as one's own.

AIDS Acquired immunodeficiency syndrome.

anesthetics Drugs given by a doctor to reduce or dull pain.

budget A plan for spending income.

cesarean birth The delivery of a baby by surgery.

condom A rubber casing rolled over an erect penis; a contraceptive.

contraception Something that is intended to prevent pregnancy.

delivery The stage of childbirth when the baby emerges from the mother's body.

discipline Training that positively shapes a child and teaches self-control.

fetus The unborn baby that is living in the mother's body.

GED General Equivalency Diploma; a diploma that is the equal or "equivalent" to a high school diploma, for people who no longer attend a regular high school.

immature Not grown-up; childish

Lamaze A method of delivery that helps mothers relax during childbirth using natural methods, without the help of drugs.

midwife A person who is trained in the delivery of babies and who is not a physician.

minimum wage The lowest rate of pay that the government allows employers to pay workers.

morals Beliefs about the right and wrong ways of behavior.

moral support Help or encouragement in making decisions or getting through difficult times.

paternity The condition of being a father.

premature Happening too soon, before maturity or full growth.

prenatal Before birth.

trimester Each three-month period of pregnancy.

Where to Go for Help

American Coalition for
    Fathers & Children
1718 M Street NW, Suite 187
Washington, DC 20036
(800) 978-DADS
Web site: http://www.acfc.
    org.com

Catholics for a Free Choice
1436 U Street NW
Washington, DC 20009
(202) 986-6093

Center for Successful
    Fathering
13740 Research Blvd., #G-4
Austin, TX 78750
(512) 335-8106
(800) 537-0853
Web site: http://www.
    fathering.org
email: dads@fathers.com

Father's Resource Center
430 Oak Grove Street, Suite B3
Minneapolis, MN 55403
(612) 874-1509
Web site: http://www.
    slowlane.com
email: frc@visi.com

Lund Family Center
A United Way Agency
76 Glen Road
Burlington, VT 05401

(802) 864-7467
(800) 639-1741
Web site: http://members.aol.
    com/LundFC/Lund.html

National Abortion Federation
(800) 772-9100
Web site: http://www.
    prochoice.org

National Center for Fathering
(800) 593-DADS
Web site: http://www.fathers.
    com

National Fatherhood Initiative
600 Eden Road, Bldg. E
Lancaster, PA 17601
(717) 581-8860
Web site: http://www.register.
    com/father

National Urban League
500 East 62nd Street
New York, NY 10021
(212) 558-5300
Web site: http://www.nul.org

Planned Parenthood
Call information for the
    number of the Planned
    Parenthood office nearest
    you.
Web site: http://www.
    plannedparenthood.org

Salvation Army
Call information for the
    number of the Salvation
    Army office nearest you.

United Way
Call (800) 411-UWAY to locate
    the United Way office
    nearest you.
Web site: http://www.
    unitedway.org

YMCA
(800) 872-9622
Web site: http://www.ymca.net

Call your local hospital and
ask for "Adolescent Services"

In Canada
Planned Parenthood
Federation of Canada
1 Nicholas Street, Suite 430
Ontario, Ottawa KIN 7B7
(613) 241-4474

Salvation Army
Call information for the
    number of the Salvation
    Army office nearest you.

For Further Reading

Arthur, Shirley. *Surviving Teen Pregnancy: Your Choices, Dreams and Decisions.* Buena Park, CA: Morning Glory Press, 1991.

Ayer, Eleanor. *It's Okay to Say No: Choosing Sexual Abstinence.* New York: Rosen Publishing Group, 1997

Colberg, Janet. *Red Light Green Light, Preventing Teen Pregnancy.* Helena, MT: Summer Kitchen Press, 1997.

Columbia University College of Physicians and Surgeons Complete Guide to Early Child Care. New York: Crown Publishers, 1990.

Eisenberg, Arlene, Heidi Murkoff, and Sandee Hathaway. *What to Expect: The First Year.* New York: Workman Publishers, 1988.

Lindsay, Jeanne. *Parents, Pregnant Teens, and the Adoption Option.* Buena Park, CA: Morning Glory Press, 1990.

———. *Teen Dads: Rights, Responsibilities and Joys.* Buena Park, CA: Morning Glory Press, 1993.

Spock, Benjamin. *Baby and Child Care,* rev. ed. New York: Dutton, 1997.

Trapani, Margi. *Reality Check: Teenage Fathers Speak Out.* New York: Rosen Publishing Group, 1997.

Web Sites

Pregnancy & Beyond Resource Guide:
   http://www.monarch-design.com/baby/
Fathers' Forum:
   http://www.parentsplace.com/fathers/index.html
Teen Pregnancy & Parenting:
   http:www.parentingteens.guide@miningco.com
Parenting Teens: http://www.qvtc.commnet.edu/classes/
   conflict/parents.html

Index

About the Author
Eleanor H. Ayer is the author of several books for children and young adults. She has written about people of the American West, World War II and modern Europe, and current social issues of interest to teenagers. Her recent topics include the Holocaust, teen pregnancy, stress, depression, teen marriage, and teen suicide. Eleanor holds a master's degree from Syracuse University with a specialty in literacy journalism. She lives with her husband and two sons in Colorado.

Photo Credits
Cover by Chuck Peterson; pp. 2, 9, 10, 17, 24, 28, 34, 38, 45, 50 by Mary Lauzon; pp. 20, 48, 53, 56 by Stuart Rabinowitz. Art on page 32 by Sonja Kalter.